Kari-Lynn Winters • Illustrated by Stephen Taylor

Gift Days

Fitzhenry & Whiteside
www.fitzhenry.ca

Published in Canada by Fitzhenry & Whiteside, 195 Allstate Parkway, Markham, Ontario L3R 4T8

Published in the United States by Fitzhenry & Whiteside, 311 Washington Street, Brighton, Massachusetts 02135

www.fitzhenry.ca   godwit@fitzhenry.ca

10 9 8 7 6 5 4 3 2 1

Library and Archives Canada Cataloguing in Publication
Winters, Kari-Lynn, 1969-
      Gift days / Kari-Lynn Winters ; illustrated by Stephen Taylor.
ISBN 978-1-55455-192-7
      I. Taylor, Stephen, 1964- II. Title.
PS8645.I5745G54 2012   jC813'.6   C2012-904072-X

Publisher Cataloging-in-Publication Data (U.S)
Winters, Kari-Lynn.
      Gift days / Kari-Lynn Winters ; illustrated by Stephen Taylor.
[32] p. : col. Ill. ; cm.
Summary: A young girl who longs to study but must run the household and look after her siblings after her mother's death gets an invaluable gift from her brother. One day a week, her brother does her chores so that she can pursue her dream of an education, just as her mother would have wanted, in this tale about overcoming obstacles.
ISBN: 978-1-55455-192-7
1. Brothers and sisters – Juvenile fiction. 2. Schools – Juvenile fiction. 3. Uganda – Juvenile fiction.   I. Taylor, Stephen. II. Title.
[E] dc23   PZ7.W4584Gi 2012

Fitzhenry & Whiteside acknowledges with thanks the Canada Council for the Arts, and the Ontario Arts Council for their support of our publishing program. We acknowledge the financial support of the Government of Canada through the Canada Book Fund (CBF) for our publishing activities.

Canada Council   Conseil des Arts
for the Arts   du Canada

ONTARIO ARTS COUNCIL
CONSEIL DES ARTS DE L'ONTARIO

Cover and interior design by Blair Kerrigan/Glyphics
Cover image by Stephen Taylor
Manufactured by Friesens Corporation in Altona, MB, Canada, in September 2012; Job #77504

FSC
www.fsc.org
MIX
Paper from
responsible sources
FSC® C016245

Dedication

For the girls who, because of their circumstances, carry the weight of the world on their shoulders. — KLW

To my wife, Sandra, and my son, Storm. — ST

Acknowledgments

This book would not have been possible without the contribution of Samuel Andema (lecturer at Kyambogo University, former president of the Reading Association of Uganda and currently the chair of the International Reading Association's [IRA] International Development Committee in Africa). Samuel helped brainstorm the ideas for this book and was invaluable with verifying cultural references. Our sincerest thanks to Elizabeth Beatrice Namazzi and Jalia Kangave, for helping us with the Luganda to English translations, and for checking our manuscript for cultural accuracy. Also, thanks to the wonderful people at Fitzhenry & Whiteside including Kathy Stinson, Cathy Sandusky, and Christie Harkin who backed this project wholeheartedly, and to Drs. Maureen Kendrick, Theresa Rogers, Bonny Norton, Dolana Mogadime, and Stephen Lewis, for their inspiring scholarship and projects in Africa. And finally, thanks to all of the people who read the work and made suggestions, especially Jonah Winters. — KLW

Nassali wanted to go to school like *baabawe* — her older brother — and the other boys in her *ekyaalo*. Every afternoon she listened as they returned home from school, talking about books and reading. She watched the researchers too, who came from far away and always wrote on the whitest paper. Seeing them made her heart pound with wanting.

Some afternoons, when Nassali thought that no one saw her, she pretended that she was a scholar at Makerere University, one of the best schools in Uganda.

Sometimes her sisters — Nakate, Dembe, and Acen — joined her, performing the student roles, but mostly they played with the wire truck *Maama*'s brother — their *kojja* — had made for them.

Kojja told her, "Prepare the breakfast, fetch the water, and take care of your sisters. After that, you can be the scholar."

Jjajja told her, as she wove *raffio* baskets with the other grandmothers, "Prepare the lunch, fetch the firewood, and pull the weeds in the *cassava* field. After that, you can be the scholar."

Baabawe told her, as he packed his book — a book that he owned — into his school bag, "Prepare the supper, fetch the dishes, and wash the clothes. After that, you can be the scholar."

Since her mother had died, Nassali had been put in charge of the household. Every day Nassali did the same chores.

That night Nassali waited for her brother to fall asleep. "I will teach myself how to read," she murmured. To keep herself awake, she bit down hard on her bottom lip.

At last, she heard his steady breathing. She crept closer, loosened his grip on the book, hid in the corner of her mud-brick home, and opened it. The feel of the rough paper brought a smile to her torn, chapped lips.

Nassali tried to memorize
each squiggle, but exhaustion
took over and she fell asleep.

Then someone was shaking her awake.

"That's my school book!" said baabawe.

"Please Matovu," said Nassali, "tell me what these squiggles say."

He didn't answer. Instead he held out his hand — waiting.

Outside, other boys in the ekyaalo were talking. "Where's Matovu?" asked one.

"Probably sleeping," joked another.

Nassali begged. "Please, I need to learn to read and write."

"That's crazy talk! You need to do your chores and look after — "

Nassali blurted out, "If Maama was still here, I wouldn't have all of these chores." She stared at the patched cement floor. "Oh, why did she have to get *slim*?"

Baabawe's eyes were soft. They stayed on her for a moment before returning to his book.

Nassali wiped her wet cheek and passed him the book. "Never mind," she said, tucking a mango into his school bag, "learn lots. Maama always said an education is the path to a better life."

The next morning Nassali followed baabawe to school. She knew she couldn't go inside because it was her responsibility to take care of her sisters. And besides, without proper shoes or a pencil she would be asked to leave — her family couldn't afford the uniforms and supplies for both her *and* her older brother.

Still, taking turns carrying each sister, she walked the sixty-minute route with the African sun scorching her forehead.

When they arrived, Nassali gave Nakate a banana-fiber ball and whispered, "Please play together quietly."

Hoping she might overhear the lessons, Nassali crept to the window and peered inside. Baabawe was sitting on a wooden bench.

Nassali could hear everything the teacher was saying. She felt so giddy she had to pinch her lips tightly to stifle a giggle.

Then, her brother looked out the window. Nassali gasped and threw herself into a tight ball. At the same time her sisters started to argue — loudly. So the teacher shooed them away.

That evening, Nassali cried, "It's not fair!
With all my chores, I have no time to learn!"
Kojja told her, "That is the way it is."
Jjajja told her, "That is the way it's always been."
Baabawe simply walked away.

The next day when Nassali woke up, the breakfast was already prepared, the water and firewood were already fetched, and the clean clothes were already drying.

Confused but thankful, Nassali gathered her sisters and went to her favorite jackfruit tree. While they played, she practiced printing squiggles with a stick in the dirt — like the ones she remembered from the book.

Then she fed her family lunch, cleaned the dishes, and waited for her brother to come home.

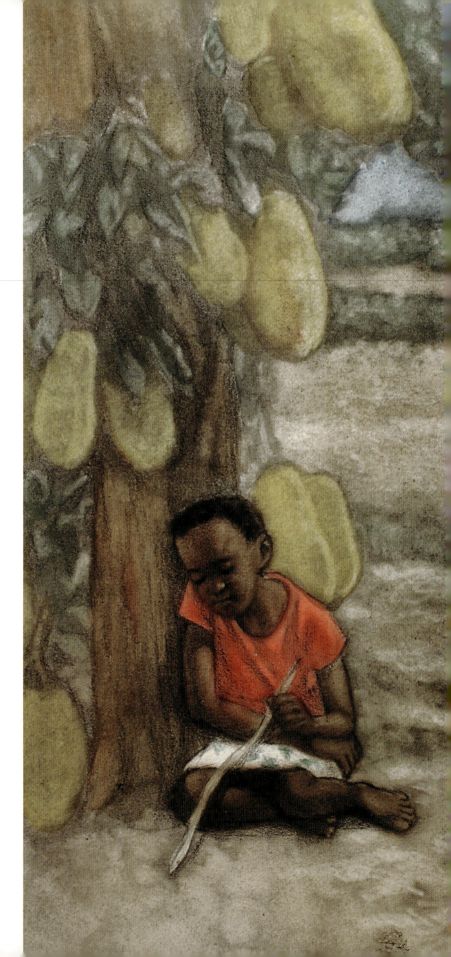

"Matovu, was it
you?" asked Nassali.
"We'll talk later.
Right now I need
to rest."

That evening, after completing their chores, Nassali and her brother sat under a jackfruit tree.

"Why did you do my chores this morning?"

Baabawe passed her his school book. "Because Maama would have wanted it this way." He pointed to the pictures and began to teach her how to read the words.

Once a week, after that day, Nassali woke up and found her chores already completed. On these special days — her gift days — she practiced reading and writing.

One evening, after many lessons, Nassali sat on the ground. She opened the book — *creak* — and smiled, inviting her sisters to join her.

Nassali ran her hand over its first page and began to read aloud to them. She was so focused on sharing the story that she didn't notice her family watching.

They gazed at each other solemnly. *Their girl, reading?*

Baabawe reminded them, "Maama would have wanted it this way."

Kojja and Jjajja nodded, showing their approval, their faces filled with pride.

Years later, after her brother
had left the ekyaalo to work as
a paramedic in Kampala,
Nassali received a letter on the
whitest paper she had ever
seen. She was accepted as a
student at Makerere University.

On this day, she borrowed
baabawe's stubby pencil and
wrote him a thank-you note on
the back of the letter.

And then she did her chores.

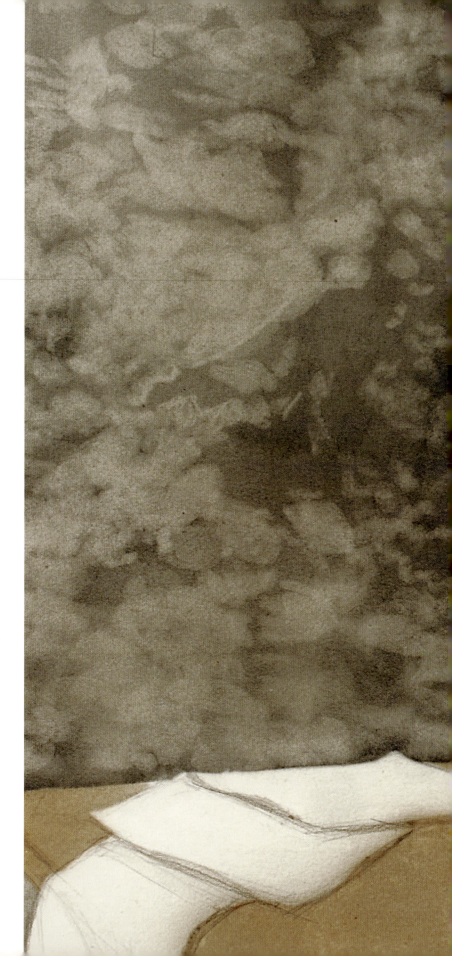

The United Nations Convention on the Rights of the Child declares that all children, no matter who they are or where they live, have the same rights. Some of these rights include the right to safe water to drink and the best health care available (Article 24), the right to play and rest (Article 31), and the right to an education (Article 28).

Many children globally do not have access to some of these basic rights. They travel great distances to get water from a contaminated source. They may miss out on opportunities to play and rest because they need to take care of their families and homes. Often, their parents simply cannot afford to send them to school or buy the medicines they need.

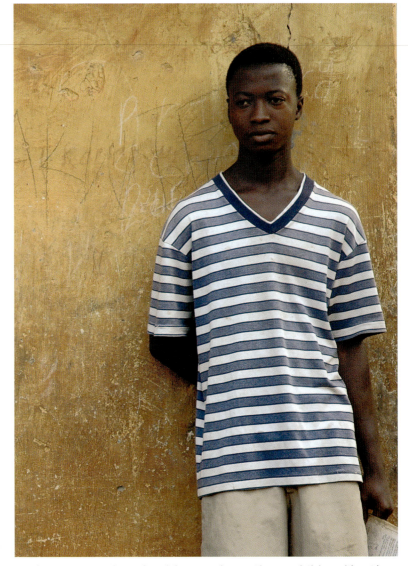

Article 28:

You have the right to a good quality education. You should be provided with an education and encouraged to go to school to the highest level you can.

Sickness, including more serious illnesses like the deadly HIV/AIDS (*siliimu*) — a virus that attacks human immune systems and is transmitted through some bodily fluids — is a part of daily life. According to the Report on the Global AIDS Epidemic (2010) there are over 34 million people living with HIV/AIDS globally. Just over a million people infected with HIV/AIDS are living in Uganda, where *Gift Days*

Without money for school fees and a uniform, children like Abu Kamara (above right) are excluded from the classroom. Like Nassali, he often spends his time outside the school walls. (Sierra Leone)

takes place. An equal number of children in this country, under the age of 18, have been orphaned by this life-threatening virus.

Girls whose family members have been infected or who have contracted HIV/AIDS themselves, especially suffer. For example, if their parents or grandparents get sick, girls are expected to stay home from school to care for them, as well as their younger siblings. Their responsibilities come first; play, rest, and even school come second. Over half a million girls in Uganda, and many more in other parts of the world, share Nassali's experience in this way.

Photos by Kathleen Martin (www.kamakwie.org)

Isotu is delighted to learn that she will be able to go to school, now that her school fees have been paid. Soon, she will have her new school uniform, too. (Sierra Leone)

Yet, schools give families hope. They provide safe spaces where children learn important skills like reading, writing, and math. At school, children also learn healthy living practices, including how to stop the spread of HIV/AIDS. And they learn how to take better care of their siblings and their own future children.

Organizations like the Stephen Lewis Foundation, Plan Canada, and UNICEF advocate for the protection of children's rights. They support children, helping them to meet their basic needs and offering them opportunities for success.

For more information:
www.stephenlewisfoundation.org/
www.unicef.org/crc/
www.becauseiamagirl.ca/
www.fitzhenry.ca/

Glossary

Ekyaalo, "village"

Raffio, "grassy fibers used for crafts and basket-making"

Kojja, "uncle (maternal)"

Jjajja, "grandmother"

Baabawe, "her older brother"

Maama, "mother"

Slim, a translation of siliimu, the slang for HIV/AIDS; a common term used in Uganda.

Cassava, "an edible plant, similar to a yam"